To Marilyn and the bookshop cats
and also
to all the cat loves in my life,
and to those I have yet to meet.

JANETTA OTTER-BARRY BOOKS

With thanks to Teague Stubbington, Zoological Society of London,
for checking the animal facts.

*I am Cat* copyright © Frances Lincoln Limited 2012
Text and illustrations copyright © Jackie Morris 2012
First published in Great Britain in 2012 and the USA in 2013 by
Frances Lincoln Children's Books, 4 Torriano Mews,
Torriano Avenue, London NW5 2RZ
www.franceslincoln.com

A catalogue record for this book is available
from the British Library.

ISBN 978-1-84780-135-7

Illustrated with Windsor & Newton artist's quality watercolours,
on Arches hotpress watercolour paper

Set in Centaur MT

Printed in Shenzhen, Guangdong, China by C & C Offset Printing Co., Ltd in May 2012

1 3 5 7 9 8 6 4 2

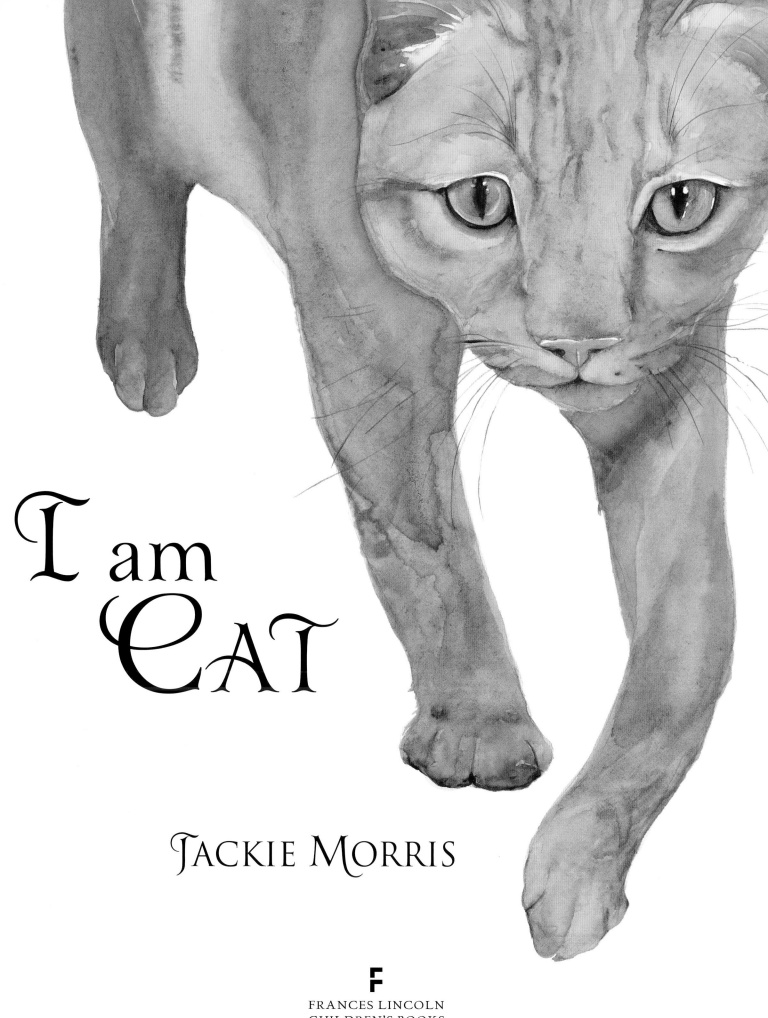

# I am CAT

## Jackie Morris

**F**

FRANCES LINCOLN
CHILDREN'S BOOKS

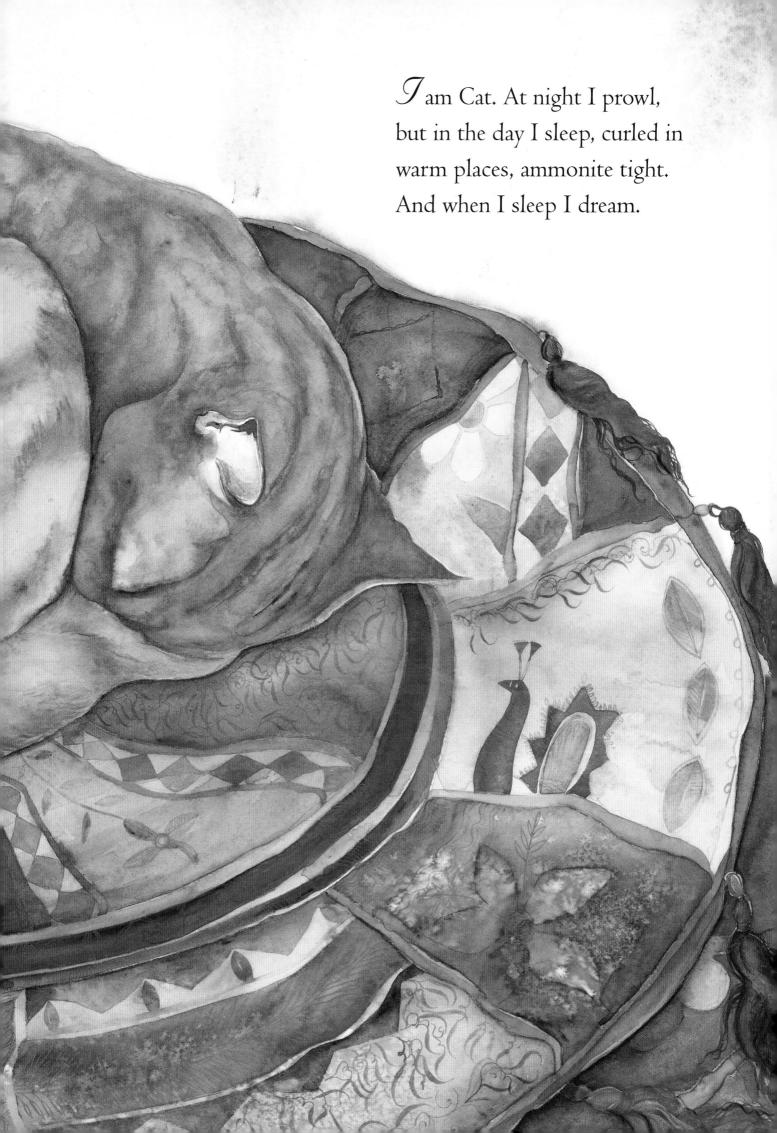

*I* am Cat. At night I prowl,
but in the day I sleep, curled in
warm places, ammonite tight.
And when I sleep I dream.

*I* dream that I roam
deep in the jungle,
bright flame-cat of the forest,
striped like the shadows,
sun-scorched.

$\mathcal{I}$ dream that I am the sharp-eyed running cat,
fast as the wind over the bleached plains of Africa,
sleek, spotted and elegant.

*I* dream that I walk
through resin-scented forests,
ears pricked for owl hoot,
nose sharp for hare scent,
a ghost in the twilight.

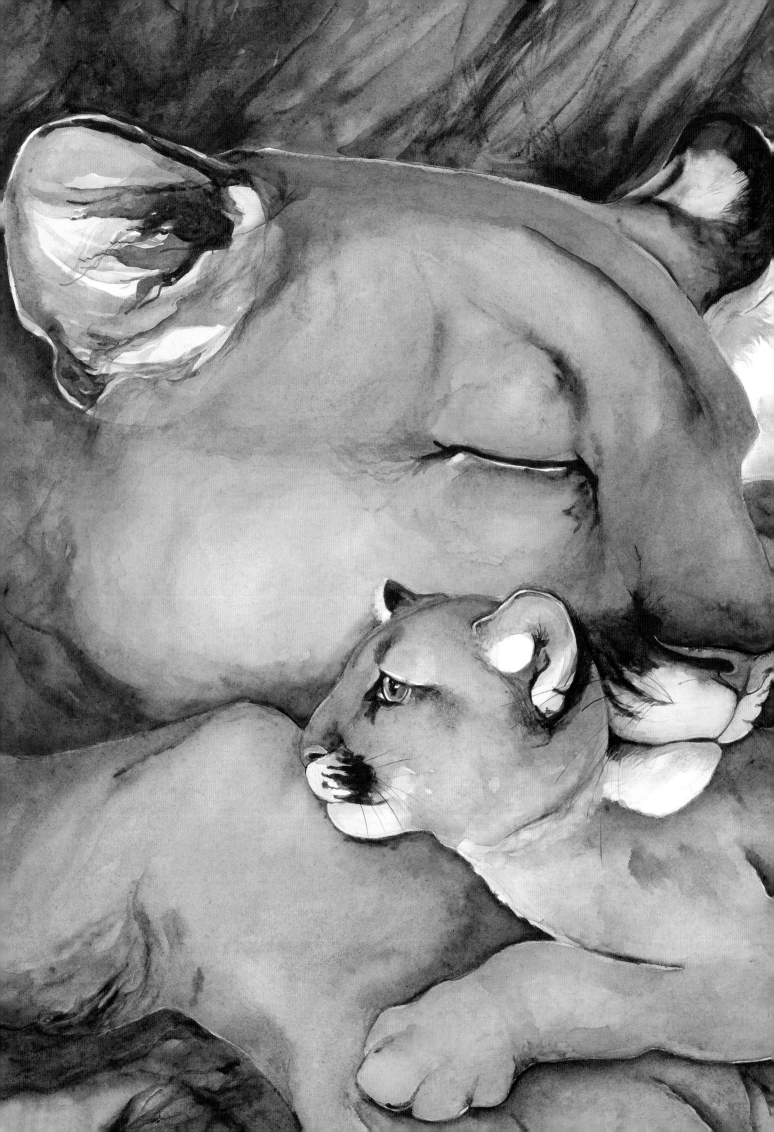

*I* dream of a cave, cubs close in the darkness,
herds of wild horses, and the need to hunt.

*I* dream that I walk on the roof of the world,
dressed in a coat of thick dappled fur,
watching, waiting. Shrouded in mystery,
coloured like the snow beneath my great paws,
lord of the high mountains.

*I* dream that I swim through warm river water.
Scarlet macaws fly over my head.
Beside me my brother, dark spirit of the forest,
coat black as midnight, beautiful.

$\mathcal{I}$ dream that I lounge through the heat of the day,
in the shade of the great spreading tree,
heavy mane tangled in sunshine, gold, like the savannah.
Around me, my pride lie sleeping
while restless cubs tumble in kitten play.

*I* dream that I am the secret cat,
wild in the mountains and forests
of Scotland. Striped like the tiger,
solitary and fierce, ancient,
almost a memory.

*I* dream that I walk through forests of Russia,
snow beneath paws. Regal, thick coat
coloured like leaves in autumn,
almost the last of my kind.

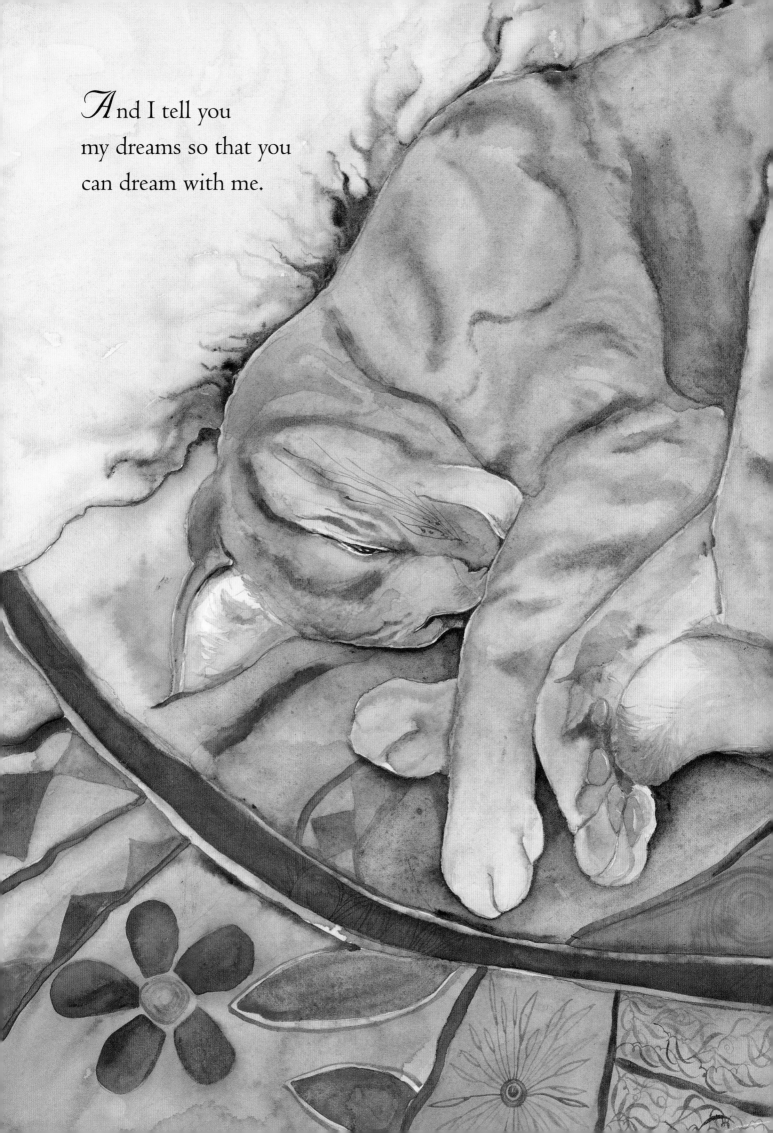

*A*nd I tell you
my dreams so that you
can dream with me.

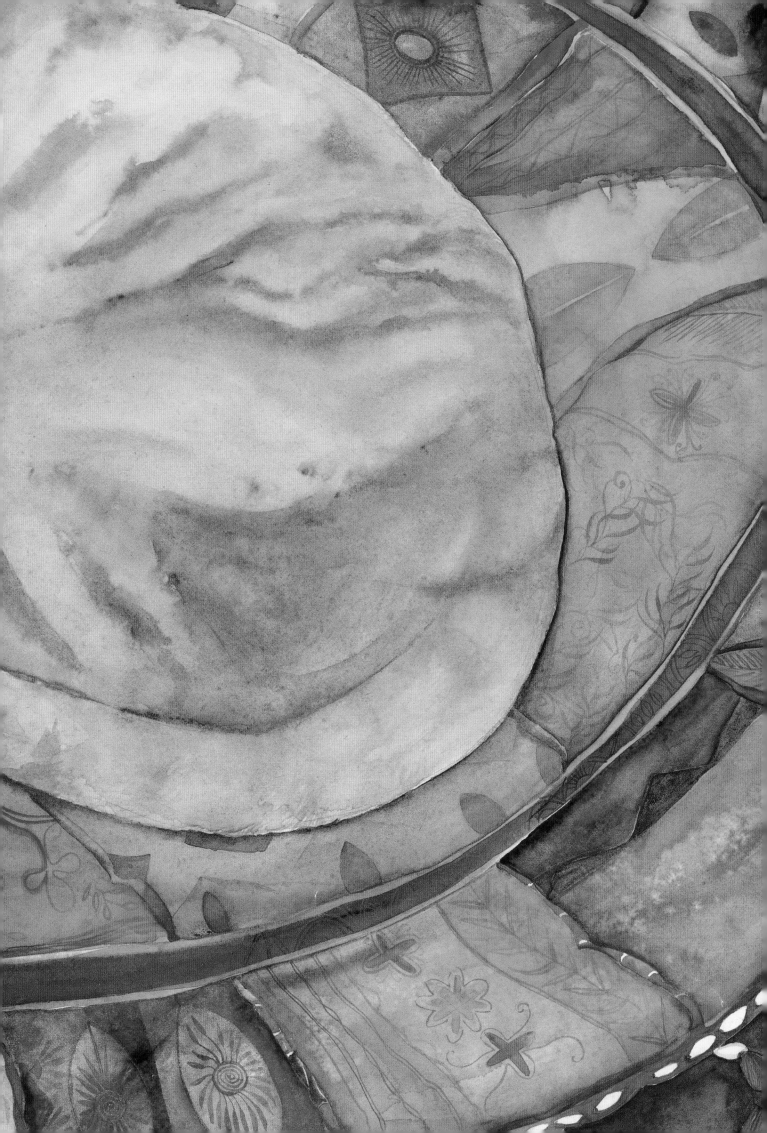

## Domestic Cat

Domestic cats are thought to have evolved from a small African wildcat. They have lived with humans for thousands of years. In China they were used to protect the silkworm cocoons from mice and rats. Cats miaow to communicate with humans and have a language of their own which involves sounds and scent marking. In ancient Egypt cats were sacred. The penalty for killing a cat was death. In India the feline goddess Sasti is said to be a guardian of children.

## Siberian Tiger

Tigers are the largest of the big cats. The Siberian Tiger is largest of all tigers, weighing 320 kgs (706 lbs). There are now thought to be only 200 Siberian tigers living in the wild, in the far east of Russia and the mountains between China and Tibet. There are probably more tigers in captivity in the world than in the wild. Tigers are striped, as camouflage. In the forests where they live they hunt at night. Tiger cubs stay with their mothers for over two years.

## Cheetah

Cheetahs are the world's fastest land animals, reaching speeds of 70 miles an hour in short sprints. They are lightly built with long legs. A cheetah is the only cat that cannot retract its claws. Cheetahs live in Africa. They give birth to their cubs on the grassland and move them every two to three days. They have between 1 and 8 cubs. Female cheetahs are solitary but males live in small groups and stay together for their whole lives. The name 'cheetah' comes from the Hindu word 'chita' or 'spotted one'. In Asia cheetahs were used by man for hunting small antelopes. They are often depicted in the beautiful miniature paintings of hunting scenes.

## Lynx

There are lynx in Europe and America, but the Eurasian Lynx is almost twice as large as the American Lynx.
The lynx is a solitary, secretive hunter. Lynx feed mainly on hare and rabbit, but will also eat small deer, birds and mice. Lynx are very distinctive with their sharply pointed, tufted ears.

## Puma

The puma is a cat with several names. 'Puma' is the name given to the cat by the Incas, long ago, in South America. 'Cougar' is its North American name, and it is also known as the 'mountain lion', although it is more closely related to the domestic cat than to the lion. Pumas range from the southernmost tip of South America to Canada. They are large, solitary cats, who like to live in rocky areas with dense bushes. They hunt alone, and their prey includes deer, porcupine, hare, raccoon, opossum and wild pigs.

## Snow Leopard

Snow Leopards have thick coats, long tails for balance and huge paws for running over snow. Their shoulders are strong for climbing and hunting in the steep mountains of Central and South Asia where they live. The Snow Leopard's call is a strange and eerie scream. Cubs are born with a dark stripe that separates into spots as they grow. Their coats act as camouflage in their mountain home. Fierce and elusive, they have inspired many legends. Snow Leopards eat bharal (a sheep-like creature). They need to make a kill every 10-15 days. If they guard their kill it will last them for several days.

## Jaguar

Jaguars are solitary cats who live in Central and South America. They eat snakes, lizards, caimans, fish, turtles, capybara, monkeys, anteaters, small deer and birds. Jaguars are important animals in South American mythology. The Mayan people believed that they guided the sun on its journey beneath the world so that it would rise again on the following day. Jaguars can be spotted, with rosette spots, or deep black. But even black jaguars have rosette spots in their coats – a deeper, darker black.

## Lion

Lions live in groups called 'prides', sometimes just a few together, sometimes up to 40. The lioness, despite being smaller than the male, is the one who will hunt and keep the pride's territory. The male uses its size to steal food from the lionesses when they make a kill. Only 1 in 5 hunts is successful for a pride of lions. Lions are found in the plains and grasslands of Africa. At one time they were widespread in Asia too, but now only about 400 lions remain in the Gir forest in Gujarat.

## Scottish Wildcat

The Scottish Wildcat is a 'true' wildcat, not a domestic cat that has become feral. Only 150 breeding pairs are left now in the wild, in the remote Scottish Highlands. Wildcats are marked like a tabby cat, but can be up to 50% larger. They have a short, bushy, banded tail. When a wildcat makes a kill it will eat everything, even crunching on the bones of its prey. Wildcats are said to hunt for fish in shallow streams, using their paws to hook trout and salmon from the water. The biggest threat to wildcats is man. Cats are shot, hit by cars and caught in snares.

## Amur Leopard

There are nine different kinds of leopard, of which the Amur Leopard is the rarest. It is the world's most endangered big cat, with less than 30 individuals left in the wild, mostly in the temperate forests of Russia. Leopard coats vary in colour from grey to brown to black. Leopards are solitary cats. They hunt alone. Threats to leopards, especially the Amur, are habitat loss and poaching. They are hunted for their fur, and their bones are used in Oriental medicines. Also their prey is susceptible to poaching.